Project: Genius

Written and Illustrated
by WILLIAM HAYES

SCHOLASTIC BOOK SERVICES

Published by Scholastic Book Services, a division
of Scholastic Magazines, Inc., New York, N.Y.

To the memory of my father,
and to my wife, Kathryn

Single copy price 35¢. Quan-
tity prices available on request.

Chapters 13 and 14 of this book are based on the story MY
BROTHER IS A GENIUS, which first appeared in The Betts Basic
Readers, Second Edition, The ABC ADVENTURES NOW AND
THEN: copyright © 1959 by American Book Co.

1st printing .   .   .   . September 1963

Printed in the U.S.A.

CONTENTS

Project?

IT WAS A BIG YEAR. Now that school is out and the State Science Fair is over, I guess I can tell about it.

After the animals broke out of their cages, the red fox cub was caught out at Mr. Sheppard's farm. The white rats were caught, too—all except Eustace. Eustace was the smartest. I think maybe he found a good home somewhere.

The broken lab windows have been fixed. Mr. Henhauser, our principal, is going to be all right, too. His trouble was mainly psychosomatic. I mean he wasn't really hurt by the explosion. Just shaken up a little, and more scared than anything, I guess. Anyway, he has gone to the mountains for a rest. Most of the kids are sure he will be back by the end of summer. I think so, too.

One thing I will say for Franklin School, they encourage outside activities. Every year our school gives a prize for the most original outside project. They encourage inside activities, too. We really have to study. The winner has to have good grades.

The prize is always a trip to some interesting place. Usually it's a historical place or something like that where everybody wants to go. This year it was a trip to the State Science Fair. Mr. Henhauser announced it in assembly the first day of school.

After assembly I said to Chet Manley, "Chet, I'm going to win that trip or bust. I have some ideas cooking for a real project."

"Oh boy, Pete! Have you?" he said. "What kind of a project?"

"A big one," I said. "And do you know what I'm going to do first?"

"No."

"First I'm going to join the Science Club. Know why?"

"No."

"So I can use the science lab after school hours, that's why. The Science Club has meetings only once a week. But Mr. Stroop lets the members use the lab just about any time they want to after school. Elmer Albertson told me so. I remember last year I used to see him in there boiling stuff and doing experiments and making all kinds of things. I've seen some of the stuff they have in there, too; and I've been thinking of ways to use some of it."

Chet rolled his shoulders and frowned the way he does when he's thinking. "I wonder if they would let me join the Science Club," he said.

"Of course they would. Why not?"

"Well, I don't know much about science. But if I could be around all those tubes and bottles and scientific things, and the fox cubs, too, and Eustace and the other white rats — if I could be around all those things — I'll bet I could learn a lot about science. I might even work up a project myself."

While Chet talked, he was chinning himself on the water pipe — the one high up by the cafeteria wall. Chet can think better when he's moving around.

"You have the right idea," I said. "Let's go find Mr. Stroop. The sooner I get in that Science Club, the better."

I knew the Original Outside Project didn't have to have anything to do with science. But the way my ideas were shaping up, I knew the lab would come in handy.

We found Mr. Stroop at his desk in the lab. He was making soft barking noises at the fox cubs. The foxes were pacing back and forth in their cage and just looking at him. I was interested in those foxes.

"Mr. Stroop," I said, "we would like to join the Science Club very much."

"Well," he said, "I am always glad when students show an interest in things outside of their classwork. But our lab space is limited. So is our equipment. We have to keep the membership down so that club members can work in here comfortably and safely. And another thing, Pete, are you sure you have time for more activities? Last year you were president of your class. You were on the debating team, too. And I believe I remember something about a committee for putting up a statue of Benjamin Franklin on the school lawn. And there was another committee to put up a monument in honor of *all* American statesmen — not just one. The two committees wrangled with each other for months and got nowhere."

"I guess they did the best they could," I said.

"But you were on both committees," Mr. Stroop said.

"I have to keep an open mind," I said.

"What I'm trying to say is that I doubt if you have time to do justice to the Science Club," he said.

"This year I'm going to devote myself to science," I said.

"Exactly what interest do you fellows have in science?" Mr. Stroop asked.

"Well," I said, "the world we live in is advancing very rapidly and the progress of technological development is very important to the whole human race and to the universe besides."

Chet was nodding his head fast before I finished. "Yes, sir, that's the reason why, all right," he said.

"And besides," I said, "I have some ideas for a project. I want to win that trip to the Science Fair. And I want to use the lab to work on my project."

After what seemed a long time, Mr. Stroop said, "Well, all right. But I'm going to expect big things of you two." He shook hands with us. "Welcome to the Science Club," he said. "Meetings are Tuesdays after the last bell."

At the first meeting Mr. Stroop talked to us for a long time. He said a lot about the Scientific Method, about questioning everything and finding things out for ourselves, about safety rules in the laboratory, and about always cleaning up the place after we made a mess.

Mr. Stroop was very firm about one other thing. All experiments and projects in the lab had to have his okay.

We worked for a while with some of the test tubes and retorts and other equipment. Chet put a beaker of water over a Bunsen burner. Before long the water was boiling.

"What are you doing?" Arnold Gastonbury asked him.

"I'm making steam," Chet said.

"What are you going to do with it?" Arnold asked.

"You don't have to *do* anything with it," Chet said. "I'm just *making* it. That's all."

"It doesn't sound very scientific to me," Arnold said.

Chet looked hurt. "You've got to start somewhere," he said.

By the end of the first meeting, I had finished sizing up our lab. There are a lot of interesting things in there besides test tubes and Bunsen burners.

When the Science Club started several years ago, Mr. Henhauser wrote a letter to our local paper. The letter said that the Science Club needed equipment to work with. The paper printed the letter, and people brought in a lot of things for the Science Club to use. Some of the stores in town gave things, too.

There is a surveyor's telescope, and a sundial, and a soldering iron, and a geologist's hammer. There is an old crystal set that really plays. You have to listen to it with earphones. And there are some old-fashioned grocery store scales. The lab has a continuous-loop tape recorder, too. It plays back over and over again as long as you have it turned on.

There were things going through my mind all through

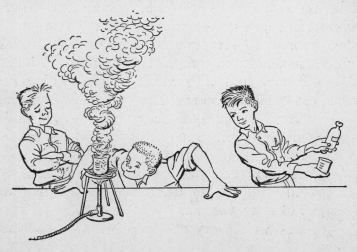

that first meeting; ideas were falling in place. And if everything worked out, I was going to need that tape recorder. The only trouble was that you couldn't control the volume very well. You could turn it down soft, but then it would creep up gradually and get louder. I looked at it, though, and I was sure I could do something about it.

The day after the meeting when Chet and I were in the lab I said, "Chet, do you realize what a person with real imagination could do with this equipment?"

"Sure. Oh sure," Chet said.

"Chet, I have an idea that ought to win me that trip. All I need is Eustace and three of the other white rats and one of the fox cubs and that continuous-loop tape recorder."

"Oh boy, Pete! How many projects you going to do with all those things?"

"Just one. But it's a big one. And it ought to be a winner. I think I'll get everything ready before I ask Mr. Stroop about it. I know he'll okay the idea when he sees how I have everything worked out."

"You think of everything," Chet said.

"I'll have to make separate cages first. One for one of the foxes, and one for Eustace and three of the other rats," I said.

Then I told Chet what my project was going to be. There were tears of admiration in his eyes when I finished.

"Pete," he said, "I'm proud to have the acquaintance-ship of a person of your caliber. Who else would have thought of what you could do with a fox cub and Eustace and three other white rats and a continuous-loop tape recorder?"

Baby Sitter

A PERSON NEVER KNOWS how much his life can change all of a sudden until there is a little baby brother in his family like my baby brother Andrew. Andrew had been born in the early summer. There was a lot of excitement about it at the time. People called up and sent telegrams all day and all night.

But by the time school started, things had settled down to normal. At least that's what I thought.

About the third week of school I came home one day and found my mother standing in front of the mirror. She was singing and trying on a hat that had a lot of feathers on it.

"Do you know what Andrew ate today?" she said, and went right on humming to herself.

"The other sock?" I asked.

"No," she said. "He ate a whole jar of strained spinach and a jar of strained prunes."

"We'll have to be more careful and keep things like that out of his reach," I said.

"You don't understand," she said. "This is wonderful. This means Andrew is growing up."

I went over to the crib and looked in. "It does?" I asked.

"Yes," she said. "And now maybe your father and I can start going out to some of the things we have been missing."

I knew my mother had hardly been out of the house since Andrew was born. "That will be a good change for you," I said. But I had a funny feeling down inside. I didn't quite know why, but I wasn't sure I wanted to find out.

Things were not the same for me at our house after that. My life was mapped out for me. And it wasn't the way I planned things for myself. It didn't have anything to do with exploring the planets in my own space ship or even becoming a rich sea captain or a fireman. My new career had nothing to do with any of these things.

I was a baby sitter.

I had to stay with Andrew while my mother and father went to P.T.A. meetings and to Civic Improvement Club and to concerts and things like that.

In one way it wasn't so bad. I had to keep up with my studies, and I got a lot of homework done on the nights I stayed with Andrew. My trip to the Science Fair was as good as won if studying had anything to do with it.

Whenever Chet or anyone wanted me to go to a movie or somewhere, if I couldn't go I just said I had homework to do. I never said anything about baby-sitting.

I would walk back and forth by Andrew's crib and read the lessons to him. I waved my arms like a windmill.

Andrew slept most of the time, but when he was awake he seemed to enjoy the lessons. He made funny noises, as if he might be trying to talk.

Sometimes I watched TV for a while, but not very often. My father has a strict rule about TV. "The studies

come first," he says. "Then if there is any time left, you can watch TV."

I didn't mind all of this for a while. But after a couple of weeks I was tired. And I didn't know how much longer I could keep my secret — the secret that I was probably the only boy in school who had to baby-sit every night. Well, not *every* night, but almost.

One day Chet Manley and Roswell Peterson wanted me to go to a movie with them that night. I knew my mother and father were going out and I would have to stay with Andrew.

"I'm going to stay home tonight and study my history lesson," I said. "And then I'll watch a good program on TV."

"But there aren't any very good programs tonight," Chet said.

"Oh no?" I said. "Did you know that Professor J. Woodly Bidhoff is going to talk over WZY about the jawbone of the Abominable Snowman?"

"No, I didn't," Chet said flatly.

"Neither did I," Roswell said.

Something had to be done.

At the supper table I tried to think of some diplomatic way of bringing up the subject. "I'm a little tired of baby-sitting," I said. "There isn't enough fun in my life."

And my father said, "I was thinking today that you have a great deal of free time, son. You have been late for supper twice this week because of your activities at school. I'm sure you spent all that time in the lab because you enjoyed it. They didn't hog-tie you, did they?"

"No, sir."

"And do you know what I had to do after school when I was your age?"

"Yes, sir," I said. "You had to work in your father's grocery store every day. And there wasn't any time for you to play or go out for sports. And as for Science Club, your school didn't have any such thing. And not only that, but — "

"And not only that," my father cut in, "but I had to work all day Saturday. And if I got to go to a movie once a month on a Sunday afternoon, I was lucky. And there wasn't any television then, either."

"Why do they call them the good old days?" I said.

That made my father laugh a little. He does sometimes when he's in a good mood.

"It isn't that I have anything personal against my little baby brother," I said. "It's just that I don't have much real companionship with him. He doesn't speak my language. I think it may be the difference in our ages."

"Son," my father said, "we all have to make sacrifices sometimes. And another thing—did you ever stop to think that the really great men of history were those who could turn a disadvantage into an advantage?"

"No," I said. "I never did."

"Well, you think about it," he said.

After they were gone I leaned on the crib and said, "Andrew, I don't know of any way to turn you into an advantage. But if I ever figure out a way, believe me, I certainly will try it."

Surging Ahead

MY PROJECT would have been ready sooner if it had not been for the baby-sitting and for the fact that Mr. Eggleston, our history teacher, was very firm. He wouldn't excuse me from history class so I could finish making the animal cages.

Mr. Eggleston is chairman of the Outside Projects Judging Committee. That's the committee that picks the best project every year.

"But it's for my Original Outside Project," I told Mr. Eggleston.

"Then you'll have to keep it outside," he said. "We can't allow any project to interfere with the curriculum."

Chet and I went to the big dictionary in the library and looked up *curriculum*.

"Here it is. It means course of study," I said.

"Why didn't he say that?" Chet asked.

"Well, it's what he meant," I said. "And I guess that's the way it will have to be. I'll do this project without letting it interfere with the curriculum."

And finally, in spite of Mr. Eggleston, everything was ready. Well, not *everything*. I still had to get permission.

"You want to WHAT?" Mr. Stroop almost shouted

when I told him my idea. He stood up, leaned forward, and grasped the sides of his desk.

"I want to find out the effect of music on Eustace and three of the other white rats and on one of the fox cubs," I said. "And I want to use that tape recorder."

I took a deep breath. "I want to turn the tape recorder on and leave it turned on so I can see how the animals react to the music."

"We can't have that tape recorder playing in here," he said. "It would disturb the science classes."

"Oh, I don't want to leave it on in the daytime," I said. "I want to leave it on all night."

Mr. Stroop sat down hard. He looked over at the cages. The foxes were pacing back and forth and watching us with big bright eyes. Eustace and the other white rats poked around their cage and didn't look at anybody.

After a while Mr. Stroop started to smile. "Well, why not?" he said. "It sounds like an interesting project."

Then he said, "You will need more cages, you know. If this is to be a scientific experiment, you will have to keep the tested animals separate from the others."

"I thought of that," I said. "I've already made the cages. I made one for the fox, and one for Eustace and three other rats. The cages are in the woodwork shop."

"How will you find out the effect of music on the animals?" Mr. Stroop asked.

"I'll weigh them," I said. "Cages and all. If the animals that listen to music all night gain weight faster than the others, we'll know that the music helps them to grow."

"It ought to work," Mr. Stroop said.

"And I've been fooling around — uh, making some adjustments on that tape recorder, too," I said. "I fixed

the volume control so it works now. It doesn't creep up
and get louder all by itself the way it did before. It's a
good thing I'm handy with tools."

"Yes," was all Mr. Stroop said. He looked a little pale.

"Boy!" I said. "Before I fixed that thing I had it on one
day and it was turned down low. Then suddenly it blared
out all by itself. It was loud enough to hear clear over in
the next —"

"I know," Mr. Stroop said. "I heard it."

"I'd like to sign out for that recorder now," I said. "I
want to tape some radio programs at home."

"All right," Mr. Stroop said. "But be careful with that
machine. You're sure you know how to use it?"

"Oh yes," I said. "I figured it all out myself."

I telephoned my mother and asked her if I could
bring Chet home for supper. He had offered to help me
tape the music.

"Well," she said, "you'd better stop by Mr. Barlow's
and get another half pound of ground meat. Who did
you say you're bringing home for supper, dear?"

"Chet," I said.

"You'd better make it a pound, dear," she said.

At supper Chet didn't say much except when somebody asked him a question.

"What do you want to be, Chet?" my father said.

Chet went right on eating and said, "Well, sir, I was
going to be a construction worker when I was younger,
but that was last year. And before that I wanted to be a
tugboat captain. But just the other day I saw an ad in a
magazine; it said if you join the Air Force you will have
a lot of adventures and get paid, too. And then I
thought if I was going to fly, anyway, I might as well be

a space cadet and go on missions to faraway planets. But when I told my father about it, he said for me to do good work in school and pay attention to what the teachers say and not to worry too much yet about when I grow up, but just let tomorrow take care of itself. But I'll probably decide to be a football coach unless I change my mind and become a salesman for a big company. Something like that, I guess."

"I see," my father said.

"Perhaps Chet would like some more meat," my mother said.

"Not just yet, thank you," Chet said. "I'm not quite through with my second helping yet."

After supper Chet and I turned on the radio in my room. We started the tape recorder going and lolled around and listened and talked. We skipped all over the dial, and played a lot of different kinds of music. We taped everything we could find. On one station a man with a loud voice sang a long piece I had never heard before. It was in a foreign language.

"What's that?" Chet asked.

"It's classical, of course," I said.

"Oh sure," Chet said. "I ought to have known that."

When we had everything we could find on radio, we went in to the TV. I plugged the tape recorder in, but then I saw that it was time for "The Adventures of Jungle Geraldine." "Let's listen to the first of this and see if we want to hear it," I said. "We've got enough different kinds of music. There's one of everything on that tape by now."

Chet and I slouched down comfortably just as the announcer finished saying, "We take you on another adventure with that fabulous, that beautiful queen of the jungle, once London's most sought-after society girl — and now — " and there was jungle music and jungle sounds.

It was a pretty good program. Jungle Geraldine saved all the animals from a mean scientist who wanted to blow up the whole jungle and build a factory there to make secret rockets. The mean scientist was from a country where they don't believe in democracy.

After the program was over Chet said, "Pete! Look! You forgot to turn off the tape recorder."

"Well, what do you know," I said. "We taped Jungle Geraldine."

"You can cut that part out," Chet said.

"I think I'll leave it," I said. "No harm in experimenting with something besides music."

At Science Club meeting that week I finally got things started. Chet helped me carry the cages from the shop. I put Eustace and three of the other white rats in a cage on the floor. And in a cage right above it on a table I put one of the fox cubs. I weighed the cages with the animals in them and wrote the weights in my notebook. Then I put the tape recorder on a chair and propped heavy cardboard around to make the sound go toward the cages. When the tape was playing soft and low, we went to the far end of the lab. We stood by the cages that had the other four rats and the other fox cub. "The volume is just about right," I said. "You can't hear the music at all from here."

"Remember, Pete," Mr. Stroop said, "you'll have to get here early in the morning and put things away before classes start."

Retreat

NEXT MORNING as I came near the school, I heard it. Mr. Henhauser was just starting up the front walk. People going by stopped and looked at the building. Music poured out of the whole building, even with the doors and windows closed.

Mr. Henhauser ran up the steps. The music got louder. I started to run, too. A loud voice was singing in a foreign language. I recognized it as part of that tape recording.

"*Toréador, en garde! Toréador! Toréador!*" the voice sang. I think it's probably from an opera.

By the time I ran up the steps and into the building the sound had changed. There was a lion roaring and monkeys chattering and elephants trumpeting and loud jungle music. It was so loud the walls were shaking.

I ran through the hall and started up the stairs. Then I heard a loud crash and a splintering of wood. "That's not part of the recording," I thought as I took the stairs three at a time. Then above all the jungle noises came the sound of somebody running.

Suddenly, what I saw made me want to run, too. My first impression was that a whole jungle full of animals was chasing Mr. Henhauser. But then I looked again. Mr. Henhauser was half running and half jumping down

the stairs. The fox cub and Eustace and the three other white rats were close behind him.

They ran by me, down the stairs, and through the hall. In another second the fox ran past Mr. Henhauser toward the front door. I didn't see where Eustace and the other rats went; but as I ran on up the stairs, I heard some girls squealing.

I ran into the lab and turned off the tape recorder. The silence echoed through the place like a cannon.

I stood there panting and looking around at the wreckage. The fox cage lay in a heap on top of what was left of the rat cage.

All I could figure out was that the fox got so scared when he heard all the noise that he threw himself against the side of his cage and knocked it off the table and onto the rat cage.

The pieces looked like an armload of kindling wood. I gathered them up and carried them to a big ash can out behind the school.

My first Outside Project was over, and I knew it. But as I walked back into school, I couldn't help laughing a little. Mr. Henhauser had looked as if he were ready to run around the world.

I stopped. There was an idea there somewhere. I wasn't quite sure what it was. But thoughts began to come.

Later Mr. Stroop said, "Pete, if you get any more ideas for projects, how about picking one that will work in the daytime?"

Old Four Peaks

I HAD OTHER IDEAS, but I decided not to say anything about them. Not to Mr. Stroop, anyway. Not just yet.

But there was no harm in telling Chet. So, later that week, after I had done some research, I said, "Chet, what shape is the earth?"

"It's round," he said.

"How do you know it's round?" I asked.

"Everybody knows it's round," he said.

"Everybody doesn't *know* it," I said. "Everybody just takes it for granted. What would you say if I told you I know a way to *prove* the earth is round? And without flying around it or going to outer space or anything like that, either. I'd just go a mile or two out of town."

"Where would that be?" Chet asked.

"To Outlaw Rim," I said.

"How can you prove the earth is round from there?" Chet asked. "I've been there," he said, "and the earth doesn't look any rounder from there than from anywhere else."

"Well," I said, "do you know what mountain is the most famous one in the whole state?"

"It's either Superstition Mountain or Old Four Peaks," Chet said. "One or the other."

"And how high is Old Four Peaks?" I asked.

"I don't know," Chet said. "But it's pretty high."

"Well, I know exactly how high it is," I said. "I looked it up in an atlas. Do you know why we can't see it from here?"

"Because it's too far away," Chet said.

"No," I said. "That isn't the reason. The reason we can't see it from here is that the surface of the earth curves, and the top of Old Four Peaks is below the horizon. Or at least below the Granite Hills that are in front."

"I never thought of that," Chet said.

"But if you go up to the top of Outlaw Rim you can see Old Four Peaks from there," I said.

"I know," Chet said. "I've been up there plenty of times."

"So have I. And there's a stone marker on top of Outlaw Rim that tells how high it is. So, don't you see, Chet? If we know how high we are on Outlaw Rim, and we know how high Old Four Peaks is, and how far it is between the two, we can prove the earth is round. It's easy."

"It doesn't sound easy to me," Chet said.

"Sure it is," I said. "I read just how to do it. All we need is a surveyor's telescope, and there's one in the Science Club supply closet. And, Chet, that's where you come in."

"Me?"

"Yes. I want you to sign out for that telescope. I'd better not ask Mr. Stroop for anything. It's too soon after — well, it's too soon for me to ask him for anything. But there's no reason why *you* can't ask for that telescope."

"Sure," Chet said. "I'll ask him. I will if you'll let me help you with your project."

"Oh, of course, Chet. I'll be glad to let you help. Tomorrow's Saturday. We can head for Outlaw Rim in the morning."

I waited in the hall and listened while Chet talked to Mr. Stroop. Their conversation went like this:

Chet: "Sir, we — I want to use that surveyor's telescope."

Mr. Stroop: "Why?"

Chet: "We — I want to prove the earth is round."

Mr. Stroop: "Does anyone doubt that the earth is round?"

Long silence.

Chet: "Well, I don't know. I guess I'm kind of mixed up right now. I'm not sure whether it's round or what."

Mr. Stroop: "Take the telescope, then, by all means. Don't leave that question in doubt any longer."

I heard them go to the supply closet, and then I heard Chet clumping toward the hall where I was waiting.

Mr. Stroop: "One thing more."

Chet: "Yes, sir?"

Mr. Stroop: "You and Pete be careful with that telescope. I want it back here first thing Monday morning — and all in one piece."

The Flat Earth

THAT SATURDAY was a very unusual day for late October. It was hot. Almost like summer. We could see the heat waves shimmering on the fields and highways as we started up the steep road on Outlaw Rim.

It took some talking, but I convinced Chet before we started that it would be a good idea for him to carry the tripod and telescope all the way up Outlaw Rim. I would carry the tripod and telescope all the way back down because I am lighter on my feet and can balance better going downhill.

Chet agreed. Chet is strong.

"Boy! What a day!" I said when we were quite a way up the side of Outlaw Rim. But Chet didn't hear me. He was trailing behind.

There is a place on Outlaw Rim that I've never told anybody about. It isn't hidden away, or anything like that. It's out in plain sight. You can see it from the road or almost anywhere in the valley if you look for it. It's a big rock that sticks out over a deep canyon. I go there sometimes when I have something special to think about, or sometimes just to sit and look out over the valley and mountains.

Anyway, I've never told anybody about it. Not Chet.

Not anybody. That's because I think a person ought to have some place where he can go once in a while that nobody knows about — if he wants to think about something, or if he wants to just look around and not think about anything.

Off to one side through the creosote bushes I could see that rock. I waited for Chet to catch up. Chet saw the rock, too, I think; for a minute I thought he was going to say something about it, but he didn't.

We walked on. "The sun sure is hot," Chet said after a while.

"It's Indian summer," I said. "That's the way it's supposed to be this time of year. There are scientific reasons for it." But to myself I admitted that even for Indian summer it was hot.

Heat waves shimmered from the rocks and from everywhere else. The mountains on the other side of the valley looked soft and fuzzy — not crisp and clear the way they usually look in the fall.

Chet trudged on with that tripod and telescope. Chet is really strong.

"This pocket camera is kind of heavy," I said.

"How much farther is it to the top?" Chet asked.

"Not too far," I said. "We're almost to Halfway Point now. There's the marker up ahead there. You can see it as soon as you catch up with me."

"Do we have to go all the way to the top?" Chet asked. "Why don't we set the telescope up along here somewhere?"

"Because we can't see Old Four Peaks from here," I said.

"Sure we can," Chet said. "There it is."

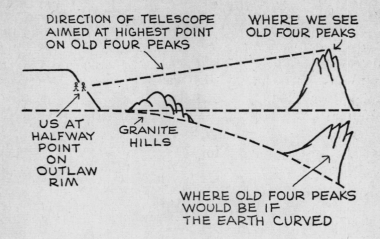

DIRECTION OF TELESCOPE
AIMED AT HIGHEST POINT
ON OLD FOUR PEAKS

WHERE WE SEE
OLD FOUR PEAKS

US AT
HALFWAY
POINT
ON
OUTLAW
RIM

GRANITE
HILLS

WHERE OLD FOUR PEAKS
WOULD BE IF
THE EARTH CURVED

I couldn't believe it, but there it was. Old Four Peaks, as plain as anything.

"Chet, it can't be," I said. "You can't see Old Four Peaks from here. It's still behind the Granite Hills. Or at least I think it's supposed to be."

"Well, there it is," Chet said.

There it was. So we set up the telescope, got it perfectly level, and sighted the highest point on Old Four Peaks. Then we took down the figures we needed. Next I clamped my pocket camera to the eyepiece and snapped a picture. Finally I backed away and snapped a picture of the whole area, showing the tripod and telescope and Old Four Peaks off in the distance.

"Chet," I said. "That stone marker over there — it tells how high we are here. How about you going over there and reading the numbers to me."

Chet called the numbers, and I wrote them down. Then I pulled out my instruction book and the figures I had looked up earlier about the height of Old Four

Peaks and the distance from Outlaw Rim. I did some figuring. I followed the things the book said to do exactly, and looked up things on the charts. When I finished, I couldn't believe my eyes.

"Chet! Come here quick!" I yelled. "There must be something wrong. Look at this."

Chet came running. "Chet, look at these figures. Do you see anything wrong?"

Chet looked over the figures. "No," he said. "But then I'm not very good at this kind of thing."

"Well, they're right! I know they are!" I said. "But if they are right, the earth doesn't curve at all, at least not down, from here to Old Four Peaks. Chet, it's eighty-eight and a half miles from here to Old Four Peaks. If the earth doesn't curve in eighty-eight and a half miles, it doesn't curve at all. Do you know what that means?"

"No."

"Chet, it means the earth isn't round. It's flat. Flatter than a flitter."

Chet thought a minute. "Pete," he said, "just between you and me, I've always suspected it."

The Word Spreads

WE DECIDED not to say anything to anybody.

Early Monday morning I put the telescope back in the supply closet before Mr. Stroop was in the lab. But as I was hurrying out, Mr. Stroop came in.

"Well, Galileo," he said, "how did it go?"

"Not too bad, I guess."

"You don't have to be modest about it, Pete. That's a good idea you had — applying the Scientific Method to an ordinary everyday thing like the shape of the earth. It's been some time since anybody came up with an idea as good as yours."

"It's been centuries," I said under my breath.

Our class was in charge of the assembly program that week, and I was chairman. When you are chairman, you have to go around to everybody and get them to do things for the program.

We aren't allowed to have anything like somebody walking a tight wire or real acrobats or a barrel race. Instead, we have to get people to do things that almost everyone can do.

It took me quite a while to get the program together, but I finally managed. Nell Halverson said she would do a Spanish dance if Elnora Bainbridge would lend her the shawl she got in Mexico last summer, and if Alice Masterson would help her do the dance and bring back the tambourine they used last time and the time before that. And if somebody would fix her castanets.

Beulah May Allston would recite "Casey at the Bat," but only if I could find her a baseball uniform like the kind they wore in 1910, or even before. My mother found one my father wore when he was a boy.

Archie Beedlewick agreed to wiggle his ears, but since you can't see that from very far away we had to give that up.

Roberta Widdemore could play very sad music on the piano, and so I got her to play "When You Come to the End of a Perfect Day" and "By the Waters of Minnetonka."

Al Barstow would sing a little. Sticky Steevers would play the accordion. He played songs like "I Wonder What's Become of Sally" and "Home on the Range."

Mr. Stroop helped us with the program. He said Mr. Henhauser had been complaining about our program's being too much on the entertainment side. He said we ought to have some serious things, too. So I asked Ardmore Reeves, who reads even more than I do, to give a talk on "Should the Eskimos Have Democracy?"

When the day came, Mr. Stroop introduced the program. I stood offstage with the list of the different acts and the names of the people who were going to do them.

I was busy checking over a lot of things to see if everybody was ready. It's always confusing at the last minute before an assembly. There are a lot of people jumping around backstage. I guess they're excited be-

cause they have to go out on the stage and do something while the whole school watches.

Mr. Stroop was at the microphone and I heard him say, "And Pete Sheldon has lined up a good program for us today. But before it begins, I want to put in a serious word for pure science. It has to do with the shape of the earth."

My stomach did a handspring.

"Not just the shape of the earth," Mr. Stroop went on, "but mainly the scientific method used by Pete Sheldon and Chet Manley to *prove* the shape of the earth instead of just taking somebody else's word for it the way most of us do. And now, Pete, I want you to tell us how you went about it and what you found."

He stepped back and motioned toward the micro-phone.

I caught a glimpse of Chet. He was shaking his head fast.

I took a few steps onto the stage. "Oh, you wouldn't want to hear about that," I said to Mr. Stroop in a very small voice.

"Step right up to the mike, Pete," he said. "Speak up. We can't hear you over there."

I didn't move. "Uh, Mr. Stroop, the program's aw-fully long already. I think we ought to — you see, the experiment — well, it didn't turn out quite like I — "

Mr. Stroop walked over to me. He smiled and put a hand on my shoulder. He led me to the microphone.

"Don't be modest, Pete," he said. "You fellows didn't lug that heavy telescope all over the country for noth-ing. Tell us about the scientific experiment. What did you find out about the shape of the earth?"

I glanced backstage. Chet shook his head and made a big silent "NO" with his mouth.

What could I do? I looked at that auditorium full of people. I took a deep breath. I thought I was going to say something about the experiment going wrong or something like that. But before I realized it, I had grabbed the microphone and yelled into it, "WE FOUND OUT THE EARTH IS FLAT."

The ringing of the microphone echoed through the whole vast room. Then for a second there was silence. But only for a second.

I thought the roof had blown off. I had never heard laughing like that in my whole life. It was so loud my eardrums vibrated. The laughing went on for a while

until it began to die down; and then it started all over
again, louder than ever.

I looked at Mr. Stroop. He was still standing with his
hand on my shoulder. The same smile was on his face.
He looked as if he had frozen that way.

We finally got through the program, but it took a long
time. Every time I went out on the stage and stepped
up to the microphone to announce something, they
started laughing again. And while the different people
were doing their acts, the tittering would start, and before long whoever was dancing or playing would be
laughing, too.

Right in the middle of "By the Waters of Minnetonka"
everyone got to laughing so loud you could hardly hear
the piano.

After the program Chet said, "Pete, let's run away and
join the Air Force."

Power!

BEFORE LONG I WISHED I *could* run away and join the Air Force. You really find out who your friends are at a time like that. I got it from all sides.

"Hey, Pete, you sure it's flat? Don't go too close to the edge now. You might fall off."

"Ever hear of Christopher Columbus?"

"Back to the Middle Ages, eh, Pete?"

I started going home every day as soon as the last bell rang. The second day my mother said, "Are you sure everything is all right at school, dear?"

"School?"

"Where you get your education, Pete."

"Oh sure. Everything's fine, I guess. Can't I come home once in a while? After all, you expect me to be here with Andrew all the time."

A couple of meetings of the Science Club went by. I didn't go. I hadn't seen Mr. Stroop up close since the assembly program. Every time I saw him coming down the hall, I ducked into an empty room or somewhere, so I wouldn't bump into him. But this doesn't mean that I wasn't busy. I had been reading. Some of my best ideas come from books. And I had been working.

One morning Chet said, "Pete, I haven't seen much

of you. It doesn't pay, staying away from the lab like this. People are getting ahead of you. Some of them are almost finished. Wilfred Strathmore the Third says he's got a project that is sure to win. Even the one I'm working on isn't so bad. I don't think you're going to get that trip this year."

"That's just what you think," I said. "I've got a project working that's a lot better than anything I ever thought of before. There's no comparison."

"You have, Pete?" That sounded like the old Chet.

"Yes. And I think this one's going to win. I guess I've really got something good this time. It's a big project. And I've already started on it."

"You have, Pete? What is it?"

"Well, it's really three things. I mean, there will be three different things in the project. The first one is pretty well along. It ought to be finished in a few days."

"Where are you making it, Pete?"

"In the basement at home."

"What's it going to be, Pete?"

"Chet," I said, "do you know what is one of the most important things in the world to modern man?"

Chet rolled his shoulders and frowned and thought a minute. "Money?" he said.

"No," I said. "Power. If it weren't for the development of power, we would be living in caveman times."

"Then we would be living a long time ago," Chet said, frowning. I could see he was wrestling with that one.

"And so," I said, "my project will be models of three important inventions that show the development of power through the ages."

"Oh boy, Pete!"

"I want to use the lab later. But I don't have to talk to Mr. Stroop about it yet — not until after I finish what I'm making at home."

"What you making at home, Pete?"

"Oh, it's just a model of an ancient catapult. The kind that could throw big rocks at enemy armies."

Chet's eyes were wide. "A catapult! And what are the other things in your project?"

"One will be a model of Watt's reciprocating steam engine. And the other will be an atomic reactor."

Chet gave a long, low whistle. "Pete," he said, "I'll never lose faith in you again. I ought to have known everything was going okay. Will they all really work?"

"The catapult and the steam engine will be real working models. But the atomic reactor will just *look* like one."

Chet looked disappointed.

"You can't have everything," I said.

"I guess you're right," Chet said.

"Maybe I'm making the catapult a little big," I said. "I made the wheels first. And since it is going to be practically a scale model, I have to make the rest of it big enough to fit the wheels."

Chet grinned. "Pete," he said, "this may turn out to be your masterpiece."

The
Catapult

Not long after that I ran right into Mr. Stroop outside the cafeteria. "Pete, you've been avoiding me," he said.

"Well — I —"

"Look," he said, "the Science Club is going to have a small exhibit. We're inviting Mr. Henhauser and all the teachers as well as the students, of course. I want them to see what we've been doing in the club. I could use your help to get things ready."

"I'd like to help," I said.

"Good," Mr. Stroop said. "I'm sorry you don't have a Science Club project ready, Pete. But there will be plenty for you to do, anyway."

"Well," I said, "there is a sort of a science project I'm working on. One part is just about finished. But I didn't actually make it *in* the Science Club." I explained it to Mr. Stroop, and he said to bring it.

We worked hard on the exhibit for a week. When things were just about ready, I got Chet to help me bring in the catapult. We had a tough time getting it up the stairs. The wheels kept rolling and it was hard to handle. We finally got it on top of one of the big tables in the lab.

"That's awfully big for a model," Mr. Stroop said. "Did you have to make it so big?"

"I guess it *is* a little big," I said.

Mr. Stroop eyed it suspiciously. "It certainly looks like a powerful machine," he said. "I'm glad it's just a model."

"Oh, it will be okay," I said. "It has a safety latch. I thought of everything."

"Safety latch! You mean this catapult is a real working model?" I couldn't remember ever hearing Mr. Stroop's voice sound as shrill as that before.

"Yes, sir," Chet said proudly. "This thing could heave a fifty-pound boulder from here to — "

"Oh, nothing like that," I said. "I just wanted to make it authentic, that's all."

"Well, it looks authentic enough, all right," Mr. Stroop said. He walked away looking over his shoulder at the catapult as if he thought it might follow him.

A little later Mr. Stroop said, "We had better release the arm of that catapult before the exhibit starts — just to make sure there's no mishap."

"But it wouldn't look the way a catapult is supposed to look if we do that," I said. "The pictures of catapults always show them like this — all ready to throw a big rock. People won't know what it is if it doesn't look like the pictures they've seen of catapults."

"Hmm," Mr. Stroop said. "Well, somebody will have to watch that thing."

It was Chet's idea to put the rock in the catapult. "You want it to look authentic, don't you?" he said. "What good is a catapult without something to catapult? This rock ought to do it."

Mr. Stroop was out of the room. "I don't know, Chet. Maybe that's being *too* authentic," I said.

I watched Chet heft that rock up and set it in place. It was a struggle even for Chet, and Chet really is strong.

"I'm just glad I put a safety latch on that thing," I said.

Discharge!

THEY LEFT EVERYBODY out of school an hour early the day of the exhibit. Some of the kids went home, but a lot of them came to the exhibit.

Chet's job was to guard the catapult. I was still helping to set up a few last-minute exhibits when people started coming in. The place filled up fast. Everybody walked around to the different exhibits and picked up beakers and test tubes and turned knobs and pulled levers.

Right in front of the catapult Orvie Welch and "Fig" Newton started pushing each other. Chet stepped between them and said, "Break it up. What do you guys think this is, a school bus?" Orvie and "Fig" went on to the next table.

"Nice going, Chet," I said. "Keep up the good work."

Several times in the next hour I caught Chet's eye. Each time he nodded his head and clicked his tongue, which meant everything was all right.

Mr. Stroop talked to the other teachers and explained the scientific things in the exhibits. It was getting late when the crowd began to thin out.

Finally there were just a few of the teachers and Mr. Henhauser. Mr. Henhauser walked around looking at the exhibits and nodding. He stopped at the catapult and looked at it for a long time. Chet stood stiff and straight. Chet always does that when Mr. Henhauser or somebody important is around.

"That catapult certainly looks like the real thing," Mr. Henhauser said. Chet loosened up and started to say something; but I waved my arms and shook my head, and Chet kept quiet.

Mr. Henhauser walked around the catapult several times. He thumped it in a couple of places and patted the wooden sides. While he studied the catapult, he studied Chet, too, as if he thought Chet was part of the exhibit. Mr. Henhauser poked around the catapult for a long time. I could see that Chet was worried, but Mr. Henhauser didn't touch the safety latch. In a little while he moved on to the next table, where Arnold Gastonbury was working an apparatus to show that fire has to have oxygen in order to burn.

Chet gave a sigh and leaned against the catapult. It started to roll, but Chet grabbed it and steadied it.

After a while only Mr. Henhauser, Mr. Stroop, Chet, and I were in the lab. I whispered to Chet, "As soon as Mr. Henhauser leaves, I'll talk to Mr. Stroop about the rest of my project. I think he'll like the idea of the steam engine and the atomic reactor. He's in a good mood right now. The exhibit went fine."

I heard Mr. Henhauser say to Mr. Stroop, "The Science Club has done a splendid job. I'm in favor of doing everything we can to encourage scientific experimentation. These young people are the very future of our country. Everything depends on them. They are the very — the very —"

"I'm glad to hear you say that," Mr. Stroop said. "I

certainly agree that the school, and also the community, should do everything it can to help develop scientific young minds."

"Oh, absolutely," Mr. Henhauser said.

"For example," Mr. Stroop said, "take Pete Sheldon and his experiment to show that the average citizen can *prove* the shape of the earth without taking somebody else's word for it. I don't know what went wrong with his calculations, but the basic approach should be encouraged — the inquiring mind."

"Well, I — " Mr. Henhauser said.

"And if I had my way," Mr. Stroop went on, "we would send young people like Pete to the State Science Fair to talk to scientists from all over the world, to exchange ideas, to listen, to learn — yes, even to teach."

"Even to teach?" Mr. Henhauser asked.

"Even to teach," Mr. Stroop said.

Something peculiar was happening to the corners of Mr. Henhauser's mouth. "To teach that the earth is flat, perhaps?" he said. The buttons on his vest were jumping up and down; I think he was laughing.

They had stopped by the catapult, and once or twice Mr. Stroop slapped the table to emphasize what he was saying. Chet and I moved toward the catapult.

"Yes, something went wrong with Pete's experiment," Mr. Stroop said. "But the shape of the earth isn't important here. The important point is that every young person should try to find the answers for himself — yes, even when the answer goes against established tradition."

Mr. Henhauser rose way up on his toes and stuck his chin out. "The shape of the earth is not established tradition," he said. "It is established fact. It is not flat.

It is round. Well, not perfectly round, of course. Rotation, you know."

Then Mr. Henhauser's voice got very even and quiet. "We must be very careful of the person we send to represent our school," he said. "Do you realize there will be important people at that fair from the four corners of the earth?"

"From where?" Mr. Stroop asked.

"From the four corners of — now, see here! That's just a figure of speech. When I say four corners of the earth, it doesn't mean — you know I don't think — I was just — just — "

Mr. Henhauser stopped and took a deep breath. "Why, anything would be better than sending someone to that fair to tell people the earth is — Why, I'd rather send this catapult, this unimaginative representation of a crude machine of primitive warfare." He slapped his hand against the catapult, and the wheels started to roll.

"Chet! Quick!"

But the front of the catapult was already off the edge of the table. The whole thing toppled.

"Watch out!" I yelled.

The front wheels hit the floor. The catapult arm sprang forward. I got a glimpse of that big rock flying toward a window. Then came the sound of shattering glass. The rock kept on going in a high curve over the athletic field. A boy was running down the field for a pass. He stopped and looked back and forth, from the ball to the rock, as if he were trying to decide which one to catch.

"No!" I yelled through the broken window. "Get out of the way!"

The boy forgot about the ball and watched the rock bounce and roll along until it hit the wire fence at the back. The fence stretched like a spring and then tightened and tossed the rock back onto the field. The rock rolled to a stop and lay there with the dust curling up around it. The boy walked over to the rock, looked at it, and scratched his head. Then he looked up at the sky for quite a while.

Pretty soon Mr. Henhauser said, "I didn't know it was loaded."

The Steam Engine

I DIDN'T GO NEAR the lab for several weeks after I rescued the catapult. But I wasn't just letting things slide all that time. I was getting the parts I needed to make the model steam engine.

This was not going to be just any working model. It would run by real steam, and would be made just like Watt's engine. Some of the parts needed to be machine-made. The cylinder and the piston, for instance. And the safety valve. I took them from an old steam engine I got for Christmas several years ago.

The old steam engine wasn't much good any more. I had traded it to George Milburn for an electric motor. Then later on I traded George eleven guppy fish and a real turtle I caught myself for the steam engine back again. Then Dennie Mullins traded me a real bayonet for the steam engine, and I traded the bayonet to Wilson McKeever for a knife that had twelve blades and a book about judo. Then Dennie wanted that knife so much he offered me the steam engine back for just the knife without the judo book. I knew a bargain when I saw one. The steam engine was mine again.

But by then it was all traded out. It wasn't good for anything except to *run*. And when something gets like that the only thing to do with it is to take it apart and make something else out of it. And that's what I did. It wasn't going to be just a steam engine any more. It was going to be a model of the most important steam engine in the world. Chet and I hunted in old shops around town for the kind of copper tubing I needed and a tank that was shaped right for the boiler.

The copper tubing was easy to find, but the tank was harder. Finally Mr. Weever, who runs one of the very best junk shops in town, brought the right one out, though; and he looked proud. "Boys," he said, "this is a remarkable tank. It used to be on an old Jenny, the kind of airplane that fought in World War I. This tank used to have two machine-gun bullet holes right through the middle of it. You can see the patches if you look close. Then it was part of the fuel system in a homemade racing car. That car won a lot of races, until one day the owner wrapped it around a tree. Mrs. Weever and I used this tank on the burner of our old hot-water heater at home for ten years, until we finally got a new heater. I guess there isn't much this tank hasn't been used for. It's a real veteran."

"That's okay, Mr. Weever," Chet said. "Pete'll make it work somehow."

Later on I said to Chet, "Well, I've got all the pieces. Now all I have to do is put them together. And the things I need in order to do it are in the lab. I'll have to talk to Mr. Stroop — whether I like it or not."

"Sure," Chet said, "go on and talk to him. He's a good guy. Tell him how important it is. He'll let you use the lab. That window's all fixed up as good as new. He's probably forgotten all about it by now."

"Maybe he has," I said.

When Mr. Stroop saw me standing in the lab with my box of spare parts and things, he covered his head and started down under his desk as if he were going to hide.

"I want to win that trip," I said. "I think this project will do it."

"Why did you bring it in pieces?" he asked. "Would it be too big to go through the door if you put it together first?"

"No, sir," I said. "This one isn't going to be very big. I brought it in pieces because I have to use the tools in the lab to put it together."

He looked over at the window that was fixed up as good as new. "I'm afraid to ask," he said, "but what is it going to be when you get it all put together?"

"Well, sir," I said, "I think the development of power is one of the most important things in the history of — "

"What is it going to be?"

"A steam engine. A model of Watt's reciprocating steam engine."

Mr. Stroop shook his head. "No," he said. "Absolutely, positively not."

"But I want to win that trip. How can I win the trip if I can't work on my project?"

"Pete," he said, "why don't you take up some nice quiet hobby like raising flowers?"

"Say, that reminds me," I said. "I read about a big meat-eating flower. It grows in the jungle somewhere. It has a sweet smell that pulls its victims to it like a magnet. And then when — "

"Skip it," he said. "Maybe you'd better not raise flowers, after all."

"This steam engine that Watt invented," I said, "it was a very important steam engine."

"Very important, indeed," Mr. Stroop said.

"Watt's steam engine saved a lot of fuel," I said. "It was much more efficient than the earlier steam engines."

"It certainly was," Mr. Stroop said.

"James Watt was born in Scotland in 1736," I said. "He went to London and became an apprentice to an instrument maker, and —"

"I am familiar with the life of James Watt," Mr. Stroop said.

"I'd like to get this steam engine put together and working, so I can start on my atomic reactor," I said.

"ATOMIC REACTOR?"

"Oh, the atomic reactor won't be a working model. It will just *look* like an atomic reactor. It won't be a real atomic reactor at all."

"I'm glad," Mr. Stroop said.

I couldn't think of anything more to say. So I just stood there looking down at that box of engine parts.

"How big is this steam engine going to be?" Mr. Stroop asked.

"Not very big," I said. "See?"

He poked around in the copper tubing and things. "It certainly looks harmless enough," he said. "But what will it do when you get it all put together?"

"When I get it all put together," I said, "it will remind people that James Watt gave the world one of the most important, one of the finest, one of the —"

"All right," he said. "Get it together. Just be careful, that's all. And don't talk about it all over school. The less publicity your projects get right now the better."

Explosion!

IT TOOK A LOT OF TIME and work to get that steam engine together just right. I had to put some parts of it together a lot of times.

When the days got shorter and winter really set in, I had to go home right after school almost every day. There was always something I had to help with around the house, in addition to my usual baby-sitting chores, of course. Andrew was still keeping my grades up.

Just before the Christmas holidays I signed out for the old soldering iron somebody had donated to the lab. That soldering iron was just what I needed to put some of the parts of the steam engine together. But during the holidays I didn't get much done on the steam engine. There were other important things that kept coming up.

About the time I thought I had seen everybody's presents, Chet said, "Did you see Elmo Turley's new bicycle?" And of course I had to see Elmo's new bicycle.

"That's a good bike, Elmo," I said, after I had tried it out around the block a few times. "Did you see the skates old Art Weedon got?"

"Sure," Elmo said, "but old Art's skates haven't got rubber tires. You ought to see Bert Hartley's skates. They've got rubber tires."

And then I had to see Bert's skates, and Bert told me about somebody who got the biggest chemistry set in town. And that's the way it went.

After we got back to school, a lot of other things kept coming up. Andrew for one. My mother and father went to more club meetings than ever, and as usual I was stuck with Andrew. He was beginning to shape up, though. He was growing fast, and seemed to be a lot brighter than most babies his age. Or maybe I was just getting used to him. Andrew was good-natured and laughed a lot, and he seemed to understand what I said.

So between the short winter days, and staying with Andrew, and studying, the steam engine didn't get finished as soon as I had planned.

There was the smell of early spring in the air by the time I got that engine all put together. Finally I was ready to try it out. One day at Science Club meeting I lit the burner and got the boiler all steamed up. Everybody stood around waiting.

"It'll get going any second, now," I told them. But it didn't budge. The safety valve started blowing off steam and that was all that happened.

"Well, I guess I'll be going," Arnold Gastonbury said. And before long the others guessed they would go, too.

"Why don't you make something else?" Chet said. "There are lots of things you could make. You don't have to make a steam engine. How about a historical automobile? Like the Model T. The Model T had power. Or an early airplane. You could probably even make one big enough to fly in. You could — "

"Not in this laboratory," Mr. Stroop said.

"No," I said. "I'm going to make this steam engine work. If Watt did it, I can, too."

Within the next few weeks I took that engine apart and put it back together again five times. After the last time it finally began working.

"Boy! Look at that thing go," I said. But there wasn't anybody there to hear me or to look at it go. Except me.

When Fulton's steamboat split in two and plunked down to the bottom of the river, I'll bet people were lined up for miles watching the whole thing. And then when he got it figured out and everything was working right, there probably wasn't a soul around to see it except him. When you finally get things all figured out and everything is working the way it ought to, those are the times you seem to be all by yourself.

I stood there and watched it run for a while. Then the safety valve started sounding off, and the engine slowed down. Too much steam was coming out through the safety valve. There wasn't enough steam left to run the engine right.

"I can fix that," I said to myself. "A simple adjustment on the valve will do it. It's a good thing I'm handy with tools." And before long the engine was running fast and smooth.

Last of all was the atomic reactor. It was easier to make because it wasn't a working model. It just *looked* like an atomic reactor.

When it was finished, all I had to do was write up a report and tell why I chose this project and how the catapult and the steam engine and the atomic reactor all had something important to do with the development of power.

The day I finished the atomic reactor there was a meeting of the Science Club. After the meeting Chet and I were talking while we cleaned up around the lab. "Tomorrow's the day," I said. "I'm going to write my report tonight and turn it in to Mr. Eggleston tomorrow. Will you help me bring in the catapult, Chet? I can handle the steam engine and the atomic reactor okay."

"Sure, I'll help," Chet said.

"I'll explain everything in my report," I said. "I want Mr. Eggleston and the other judges to know that the catapult really works. The steam engine, too."

"You won't have to tell them about the catapult," Mr. Stroop said. "They already know it works."

"I hope the judges will be impressed when I turn my project in early," I said. "It's quite a while before the deadline."

"They're already impressed," Mr. Stroop said. "They saw that window before it was fixed." He went out the door shaking his head.

"What are you going to do after you turn in your project?" Chet asked. "You won't have anything much to think about."

"Oh, I'll go to school and to movies and watch TV and read some good books and study and work around the house and loaf. Things like that. There'll be plenty to do."

Chet gave a long sigh. "It's a real letdown, though," he said. "Your project is all done, and I've given up on mine. I miss the old days when something was always cooking."

"Those were the days, all right," I said. "But a person has to settle down sometime."

"Yeah," Chet said.

"Now take this steam engine of mine, for instance," I said. "It was work. Hard work. And it still looks unglamorous, but it works."

"Yeah," Chet said.

"Might as well put things away and get going," I said. "I'll grab the atomic reactor, and you grab the steam engine. We'll put them in the supply closet for tonight."

Chet picked up the steam engine. "By the way," he said, "did you ever see how fast this will go?"

"Not really," I said. "But I had it going pretty fast after I fixed that safety valve."

"You did?" Chet said.

"Yes," I said. "It steams up fast, too. Here, I'll show you."

Chet put the engine back on the table, and I lit the burner. "Mr. Stroop just went down the hall," I said. "He will probably be back in a minute. He hasn't seen it run yet, either. Might as well give it one more whirl before I turn it in."

The engine began to make hissing sounds. The piston rod moved a little. Before long the crossarm was going so fast it looked like a blur.

"Boy! It sure purrs, doesn't it?" Chet said.

"The safety valve will probably start blowing off steam any second now," I said. "I fixed it just right. This engine really builds up pressure."

Just then Mr. Henhauser stuck his head in the door. I guess he was looking for Mr. Stroop. When Mr. Henhauser started to leave, he saw my atomic reactor on a table by the door. He stepped into the lab.

I walked over to where he was. "That's my model atomic reactor, sir," I said. "I have two other models to go with it."

"Did you — did you say — atomic reactor?" Mr. Henhauser asked.

"Yes, sir," I said.

I kept listening for that safety valve; I knew it was just about time for it to sound off. Mr. Henhauser could see I was fidgety about something.

"It isn't a *real* atomic reactor, is it?" he asked. "It *is* just a model, isn't it?" He was nodding his head and looking at me in a pleading way. "I mean it isn't a real *working* model, is it? It won't — ?"

I could hear the steady hum of the steam engine. There was no sound of the safety valve. The engine had never gone so fast before. I knew I'd better do something to that safety valve.

I took a step back toward the steam engine. The whirr was steady and loud. Something had to be done quick.

"What *is* the matter with you?" Mr. Henhauser asked. He stared down at the atomic reactor. "This isn't a real — ? You wouldn't — ? You didn't — ? Good Heavens!"

I ran toward the steam engine. But suddenly I stopped. There was a peculiar sound. The whirring reached a high pitch, and then the engine jammed. The piston stood stock-still. There was something about the sudden silence that warned me. I wasn't going any closer.

I just had time to yell, "Look out!"

Chet dived under a table.

So did I.

Mr. Henhauser hit the floor. Hard.

Half a second later it came — a loud PFOOM! and a shattering of glass.

I waited a few seconds. "You okay, Chet?" I asked.

"Sure. You?"

"I'm okay," I said. "Mr. Henhauser, are you — great guns!"

We ran over to him. Mr. Henhauser was lying very

still. I took hold of his arm and shook him a little. He started to move.

"Mr. Henhauser! Mr. Henhauser!" I yelled. "Are you all right?"

"He's trying to say something," Chet said.

"Atoms! Atoms! Atoms!" Mr. Henhauser muttered.

He tried to get up, and Chet and I helped him. Then, with Chet under one arm and me under the other we helped him out of the lab and down the stairs. "I'll be all right, boys," he said when we got him to his office. We left him sitting on a couch sipping a glass of water.

Chet and I ran back to the lab. We stopped just inside the door. Mr. Stroop stood with his back to us and his hands on his hips. Steam poured up from everywhere. Two windows were smashed.

Mr. Stroop didn't even look around to see who had come into the lab. "Pete," he said, "you certainly are rough on windows."

Project: Brother

O NE DAY about two weeks later I was shuffling home with my hands in my pockets staring at the sidewalk. Chet caught up with me. He walked along without saying anything for a while. Then he boomed out cheerily, "Pete, Old Boy, what projects you got cooking?"

"No projects," I said. "Nothing's cooking."

A little farther on Chet said, "Old Art was telling me about this movie at the Majestic. It's about two bums that just knock around all over the world. They've got this pet billy goat that gets them into lots of trouble. They all get on the wrong boat by mistake and end up practically at the South Pole. Old Art said it's really hilarious. He was rolling in the aisle. Old Art wants to see it again. How about let's all go tonight, Pete. Come on. It's a great picture."

There wasn't much homework I had to do that night, but there was plenty I could do if I wanted to. "Well, I don't know, Chet," I said. "Sounds good, all right. I'll see what the situation is at home."

As soon as I walked in the house, I knew there wasn't much chance of getting to a movie that night. My mother was hurrying around fixing an early supper. I knew what that meant. They were going to a meeting or something. I would have to stay with Andrew.

Suddenly I wanted to see that movie more than I wanted anything.

When we were at the table, my father said, "Your mother and I have a very important meeting tonight. You'll have to stay with Andrew."

"I had planned to go to a terrific movie at the Majestic," I said. "It was recommended to me very highly."

"Then I'm afraid you will have to change your plans," he said. "I'm sorry."

"But it's about these two men who go just about everywhere in the world. On expeditions, I guess you might call it. They take an animal with them all over the world. They're sort of explorers, in a way. Travel pictures are very educational."

"Your studies will be educational enough for this evening," my father said. "We wouldn't want you to overdo it, you know."

When they were ready to leave I said, "I certainly am tired of baby-sitting. Why can't we get Gwendolyn Halstead or somebody like that? She does baby-sitting for other people all the time. Or Julia Krausmeyer."

"Let's keep it in the family," my father said. "And if it bothers you to think of it as baby-sitting, then don't think of it as baby-sitting. Think of it as homework. You just happen to do your studying while your baby brother is sleeping, that's all. Fortunately there is nothing really good on TV tonight. So you have one of the finest opportunities a young man ever had. You have good schoolbooks and a whole evening in which to improve your mind."

I thought he was going to leave without his favorite

remark about turning a disadvantage into an advantage. But as he helped my mother with her coat he said, "Remember, son, the really great men of history were the ones who turned a disadvantage into an advantage."

In another minute they were gone. I stomped around the living room for a while and threw a cushion at a couple of chairs. Then I made myself a peanut butter sandwich; and after I ate, I felt better.

I took the books into Andrew's room. First I opened the dictionary and picked out a word that sounded good. "Pusillanimous," I yelled. I was studying word definitions for English. "Pusillanimous," I yelled again. "Destitute of manly strength and firmness of mind . . ." I guess a fellow has to work off steam once in a while.

Andrew made a gurgling sound and began to cry.

"Pusillanimous!" I yelled. "Go ahead and cry! Cry your head off. It won't disturb me!" He went ahead and cried. I began to feel foolish and guilty. After all, it wasn't Andrew's fault I had to stay home.

I leaned on the crib. "You see," I said, "it helps me to remember the definitions if I read them out loud." He stopped crying and reached up and tried to take hold of the dictionary. "Let's see what we can find in the S's," I said. "Salubrious, Favorable to health . . . Saltatory, Pertaining to dancing . . . Segmentation, Act or process of dividing into segments . . ." The S's seemed to quiet Andrew down. I guess they do have a soothing sound. In a little while he was asleep.

I went on reading the words aloud. Mr. Allen, our English teacher, says if you can think original thoughts and know enough words to say them, there isn't anything you can't say or do. I don't know about that, but I knew I would get extra credit in English class for learning a lot of word definitions.

I thought I might as well keep my grades up, even if I wasn't going to win that trip. In fact, I had no choice. I studied for a while and then sat looking at Andrew. I kept thinking about what my father had said. Suddenly I jumped from the chair. "Andrew," I said, "you may be a disadvantage now, but I'm going to turn you into an advantage. You're going to win me that trip — and maybe a fortune besides." I had a new idea.

The next morning at school seemed to go on forever. But noon finally came, and I called the TV station. "Yes, ma'am, it's very important," I said to the lady on the telephone. "An important Original Outside Project depends on it."

"All right," she said after a few seconds. "Mr. Barnaby will see you if you get here right away."

The TV station is only a few blocks from the school. I got there right away.

Mr. Barnaby was a very busy man. When the lady led me toward his office, she said, "Mr. Barnaby is a very busy man."

I sat in a large leather chair in front of his desk. "I'm a very busy man," he said, hanging up the two telephones he had been talking on. "What can I do for you?" He was arranging papers on his desk and writing something on a pad by one of the telephones.

I cleared my throat and said, "I want to sell my little brother. That is, I mean I think just about everybody likes babies."

"How much do you want . . . of course everyone likes babies," he said. He went on arranging papers.

"I have an idea for a TV program," I said.

"Splendid. Splendid," he said, putting the tips of his fingers together and nodding his head. "Wait a minute. What kind of an idea?"

"Well, sir," I said, "I think it is an idea that would please TV audiences."

"Fine," he said, "but you haven't told me what the idea is yet."

"Well" I said, "my little baby brother is a pretty good little brother, as little brothers go."

"Now see here! I'm a very busy . . ."

"Yes, sir. My idea would be for you to choose a baby for your TV programs. The baby could advertise products like, well, milk, for instance, or baby clothes. There are lots of things babies use."

Mr. Barnaby stopped arranging papers and looked at me. "You may have an idea there," he said. "I wouldn't have believed it, but you may have." He got up and walked around the office, holding his chin in one hand and an elbow in the other. "Yes," he said after a while. "We could have a contest and pick a baby out of all the babies in town."

"Excuse me, sir," I said, "but I think it would be better *not* to have a contest."

"Why?"

"Well, you see, sir, if you have a contest, then all the mothers whose babies don't win will be mad at you."

"Hmmm," Mr. Barnaby said.

"They might even refuse to buy the things you advertise on your station," I added.

Mr. Barnaby stopped pacing and went back to his desk. "You know," he said, "you may be right, at that."

"And so, you could just pick my little brother. He would do just as well as anyone else his age."

"How old is he?"

"Eleven months. But he's going on twelve."

"Hmmm," Mr. Barnaby said. "Let me see now. There's the Daisy Dairy that we have been trying to sell on an idea for advertising with us. And the Bittie Biddie Bye Baby Shoppe." He was pacing the floor again. "The typical baby. That's it. Typical. A baby everybody will like."

"Sure," I said, "we could take some movies of him when he's at his best."

"Nonsense, my boy," Mr. Barnaby said. "I'll talk it over with the others. If we go through with this, it will be a live show."

"But what if he cries or something?"

"All babies cry. He wouldn't be typical if he didn't. Typical, that's it, typical. The typical baby."

"Yes, sir," I said.

He patted me on the shoulder. "You know," he said, "I think you may have hit on a gold mine, my boy. I wouldn't have thought it when you came in, but I do now. There is some advantage in seeing everyone who calls. Where can I see this baby brother of yours?"

"He's home a lot," I said. "Here's our address." I wrote it down for him.

That evening Mr. Barnaby telephoned and then came to the house. After he had talked to my mother and father for a while, they took him into Andrew's room. He bent over the crib and waggled a finger at my little brother.

"Say *da*," Mr. Barnaby said, chuckling.

"Da," my little brother said, grabbing for the finger. Mr. Barnaby chuckled again.

Back in the living room, he talked some more with my mother and father. "It's settled then," he said as he was leaving. "Be at the station with that fine baby a week from Saturday at ten-thirty in the morning."

Then Mr. Barnaby said, "We will pay you for Andrew's first appearance. And if the program goes over well, there's a long-term contract in it for you. 'Growing Up With Andrew,' we might call it. The program could go on for years. There's no limit to the possibilities."

"Boy! What a project!" I thought. "I can't lose with a project like this."

A week from Saturday seemed a long way off. I read a lot so the time would go faster. I even found that studying made the time go faster sometimes. The word definitions were helping my grades in English, too. I read a lot of them out loud nearly every evening. If

Andrew was fretting when he should be sleeping, I just turned to the S's and started reading. In a few seconds he would fall asleep. He seemed to like the history lessons, too; but his favorite was the dictionary.

When the day came at last, my mother dressed Andrew in a new outfit and stood smiling down at him. "Say," my father said, "I thought he was supposed to be typical. You've dressed him like a king."

He did look pretty good, all right. I couldn't help feeling proud.

When we were almost ready to do, I leaned over the crib, pointed a finger at Andrew, and said, "Say *da*."

Clearly and distinctly Andrew said, "Pusillanimous."

At first I just looked at him. "Pusillanimous?" I asked. "Did you say pusillanimous?"

"Salubrious," he said, also clearly and distinctly. He didn't slur a syllable.

"Mother! Dad!" I yelled. "Andrew isn't typical! He's a genius! We've got to call the TV station!"

"Preternaturalism," Andrew said.

I ran to the telephone and dialed the station. While I waited, Andrew said, "Semipalmate." When I told the lady who I was, she said, "Mr. Barnaby is a very busy . . ."

"I know, ma'am," I interrupted. "But this is very important. Very, very important, in fact."

"Mr. Barnaby," I said at last, "Mr. Barnaby, do you know what Andrew just said?"

"Never mind that," he said. "Get that fine baby over here right away. We're setting up lights and cameras."

"But, Mr. Barnaby," I said, "Andrew just . . ."

"Get him over here!" he shouted. "I'm very busy."

Result: Genius

O<small>N THE WAY</small> to the station I kept telling my mother and father what had happened. "We've got to tell Mr. Barnaby," I said. "This baby is *not* typical."

"I never thought he was typical," my mother said. There was pride in her voice.

At the station Mr. Barnaby rushed us into the studio and pushed Andrew's crib under one of the big cameras. There were spotlights and floodlights and cables everywhere.

"That's the control room there," my father said. It was the glassed-in part along one whole side of the studio. Two men behind the glass were signaling to each other and one was pointing to the clock.

"I think we should tell Mr. Barnaby," I said to my mother.

"Never mind," she said firmly. "He'll find out soon enough."

Mr. Barnaby rushed around giving orders to lighting technicians and camera men. When he was satisfied that there was enough light on my little brother, he bent over the crib.

I held my breath. In a few minutes they would be on the air.

Mr. Barnaby waggled a finger at Andrew and said, "Say *da*."

"Pusillanimous," Andrew said, loudly and clearly.

Mr. Barnaby stood up, still holding the finger over the crib. His face went pink and then red. "Pusillanimous?" he cried. "Pusillanimous? What does this mean?"

"Pusillanimous," I said automatically, "means destitute of manly strength and . . ."

"I don't mean that!" Mr. Barnaby roared. His hands were clenched. "This baby isn't typical," he wailed, looking helplessly at one technician and then another.

"Salubrious," my little brother said. And right after that he said, "Presumably."

Mr. Barnaby looked at me. "You!" he said. "You!" His feet were wide apart. He pointed at me. "You!" The pointing finger went up and down with his heavy breathing.

I backed away. "I didn't mean . . . That is, I tried to tell you, sir."

Mr. Barnaby slumped into a chair. "In five minutes we go on the air," he said, "with the 'typical baby.' Typical! Ha!" He flung his arms high. They fell limply to his sides. Then he slumped still farther.

"Sir," I said, "is there a dictionary here?"

He nodded and pointed to the door. "Front office. Miss Simpson," he said, staring at the floor.

I dashed through the door, found Miss Simpson, and was back with the dictionary in a few seconds. I held the book over Andrew's crib and opened to the S's. "Listen to this," I said, as calmly as I could.

"Grappling hook," Andrew said.

I started to read. "Seemly, see-saw, seething, seize,

selenide . . ." Andrew made a few gurgling noises and
closed his eyes. I went on reading, and when I looked
down again he was asleep. Someone crammed a script
into Mr. Barnaby's limp hand, and it made me feel good
to see him gather himself up slowly and look around.
Suddenly he jumped up and stepped in front of the
cameras. He straightened his necktie. A light flashed
over the control room and there was a blare of music. At
first I thought the noise would wake Andrew, but he
went on sleeping. The S's had done it.

I don't remember what Mr. Barnaby said during the
program; but I remember the cameras moving close
to the crib and Mr. Barnaby bending over and saying
soothing things to Andrew — but not too loudly. I remember he said things like "a typical true son of our
fair city," and "a possible future president." There were
tears in Mr. Barnaby's eyes as he finished his speech.
His voice was drowned out by a loud blare of "Rock-a-
Bye-Baby," which woke Andrew, but by then the program was over, anyway. Mr. Barnaby showed us to the
front door, patting his face with a large handkerchief.

When we were outside the station my mother was
smiling broadly. "It serves him right for calling a child
of *mine* 'typical,' " she said.

My father folded the check Mr. Barnaby had given
him. "This is the only check Andrew will ever get from
this station," he said. "But it will be a start on his college
education fund — though I'm not sure he'll need it."

And Andrew said, "Pusillanimous."

"Andrew," I said, "you talk too much. You just talked
me out of the finest project of the year."

Mirage

THERE WASN'T MUCH TIME. Just a few more weeks of school. Somebody was going to win that trip, and it wasn't going to be me. Not the way things were going.

One morning on the way to school Chet said, "Pete, Wilfred Strathmore the Third says his Original Outside Project is just about finished. Some of the kids have turned theirs in already."

I looked around at the grass and the green trees. The sun was hot. To myself I said, "Maybe it's just an early spring. That happens sometimes. Maybe there is still enough time. Maybe I can come up with something. Maybe I can still win that trip. Maybe I — "

"Some of those kids worked all year on their projects," Chet said. "I'll bet some of the projects are terrific. Not as terrific as yours would be if you turned one in. But pretty good, at that."

There is always a different feeling in the air those last few weeks of school. It isn't just the warmer weather, either. There are programs and special assemblies and track meets and class plays, and everybody is on lots of committees.

There is something else about those last few weeks, too. It happens every year. The boys can't wait for school to be out for the summer so they can go swimming every day and camping or just loaf around. But the girls get all choked up and sentimental about being away from school all that time.

When Chet and I got to school that morning, we wandered around to see who was there. I heard Gwendolyn Halstead say to Margaret Allerton, "Oh dear! Oh no! For the whole *summer?* Will you *write* to me? Will you write to me every *day?* What will I *do?*"

Several other girls gathered around. There was a flutter of handkerchiefs, and there were real live tears. The girls dabbed at their eyes and then they all walked away with their arms around each other.

Chet and I stood and stared. "Chet," I said, "that settles it. I tried not to believe the grass and the hot sunshine and the green trees. But this is different. When girls act like that, it's spring. Real spring."

"What do you mean, Pete?"

"I mean I haven't got much time, and I don't think I've got much chance of winning that trip. But I'm not going to give up without one more try."

"Is your project something big? Will it go fast or shoot a long way? What's it going to be, Pete?"

"It has already been," I said. "And I'm going to write a report on it and turn in the report."

"Oh," Chet said.

"Yes," I said, "maybe Andrew didn't get to be a big TV star and make me rich like I wanted him to; but he didn't do too badly for a very young person, just eleven months old going on twelve."

"Andrew did the best he could," Chet said nobly.

"Chet," I said, "I'm going to write up a report of

how I got Andrew on that TV program and what happened. And I'm going to turn in that report for my Original Outside Project. And if I don't win that trip, it won't be because I didn't try."

"Wilfred Strathmore the Third says his project is a cinch to win that trip," Chet said. "He's going to turn it in pretty soon."

"Has Wilfred Strathmore the Third heard about all the words I learned for extra credit in English class this year?" I said. "I'm going to write that report about Andrew and the TV show and I'm going to use every big word I learned this year and look up some more besides. The judges will have to give me that trip just for the big words alone."

That week end I wrote my report. First the title:

The Story of a Veritable Genius at the Age of Merely Eleven Months, but Going on Twelve, and How It Got on a Television Presentation with My Assistance.

The title was a little long, but I couldn't figure out any way to make it shorter without leaving out something.

I started the report, "In ages of antiquity, by which I mean the predawn era of modern civilization, before the miracle of television sets, now universally owned by just about everybody, a young genius eleven months old, but going on twelve, who is my little juvenile brother Andrew, might never have come to the notice of public attention."

I felt pretty good.

"Because this young juvenile genius slumbered peacefully throughout the entirety of the program, what the television audience in its blissful ignorance, being absolutely innocent about what transpired just before

the program was transmitted out over the ether waves to the anticipating audience, did not know was that my baby brother had started saying words as long as your arm, and plainly, too, in a manner clearly designed to be understood."

The words got longer, and so did the sentences. On Sunday night I read back over it all. I felt a sinking feeling inside. I was on the wrong track.

What I needed was not big words. What I needed was inspiration. That was it. And I knew where to go for that — the big rock on Outlaw Rim.

The next day was a long, hot day at school, but finally the last bell rang and I was on my way. I took a pen and a notebook full of paper and headed for Outlaw Rim.

By the time I got to the big rock, it was in the cool shade; for a while I just sat and looked out over the valley. Heat waves were shimmering on the fields and highways around the town. Lizards skittered through the creosote bushes.

I opened my notebook. First the title:

How I Put My Baby Brother on TV

Then I held the pen above the paper. "Okay, inspiration, let's go," I said. I looked down on the valley and waited.

The inspiration I waited for never came. Something else did. There is a kind of mirage we see sometimes around here. Heat waves come up from a field or a paved road and reflect the sky and trees and other things around. This makes it look as if water is flooding the whole place.

And that was what I saw out toward Apache Junction. The mirage made the highway look like everything was flooded for a couple of miles.

Mirage!

The word buzzed around me.

Mirage!

It wouldn't go away. I couldn't stop thinking about it. There was an idea beating at me.

Suddenly I knew why mirages might be important. Very important.

I ran most of the way back to town to the library.

I went straight for the encyclopedia. I turned to the M's.

Mirage (*mǐräzh*) An optical illusion causing a person to see what appears to be a real object where no real object exists. Refraction of light rays under certain atmospheric conditions causes objects — such as trees, ships, mountains — to appear to be where they are not. Light rays undergo refraction when they pass from a layer of air of one density and temperature to another layer of air of different density and temperature. The combined surfaces of two such layers may act as a mirror and cause . . .

"Oh boy!" I thought. "I hope tomorrow comes soon. I've got to have that surveyor's telescope."

I started for the door.

"What's your hurry?" Miss Stidworthy, the librarian, asked as I raced past her desk.

"Mirages," I said.

"Are they chasing you?" she asked.

"No, ma'am," I said. "I'm chasing them."

The Curve

AFTER SCHOOL THE NEXT DAY I signed out for the surveyor's telescope.

"I'm afraid to ask what you want it for this time," Mr. Stroop said. "Just be careful with it, that's all."

I looked everywhere for Chet, but I couldn't find him. Already that telescope felt heavy, and I wasn't even off the school grounds yet. Chet certainly is strong.

By the time I started up the road on Outlaw Rim I was puffing like a steam engine. At Halfway Point I stopped to rest. That's where we were when Chet and I saw Old Four Peaks.

I turned and looked. Old Four Peaks was not there. With my pocket camera I took a picture from the same place I had taken one that Saturday with Chet.

I put the tripod over my shoulder and went on. The telescope was heavy and my shirt was wet with sweat.

Finally I reached the top. I looked away off in the distance. There it was. Old Four Peaks. And it was no mirage this time. It was the real thing. And right where it ought to be.

I set up the telescope by the stone marker that said,

Elevation at this point, 2,192 feet

I snapped a picture of the telescope and the marker with Old Four Peaks off in the distance. Then I aimed the telescope at the highest point on Old Four Peaks. I clamped the camera to the eyepiece and took another picture.

I wrote down at what angle the telescope was pointing. Then I did some figuring, using the same book I had used before.

"OH BOY!" I yelled. "IT CURVES! THE EARTH CURVES! FIFTY-NINE FEET BETWEEN HERE AND OLD FOUR PEAKS! FIFTY-NINE FEET!"

"FEET — feet — feet — feet — " an echo came at me from somewhere.

I wanted to run back to town and tell everybody. But with that telescope over my shoulder the best I could do was a fast walk.

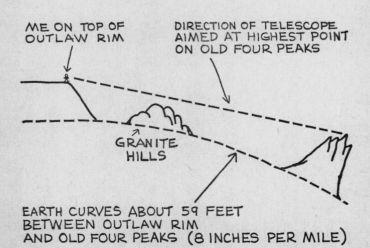

The sun was setting by the time I got back to town. I was going past the Majestic theater where they always have at least two features and sometimes a travel picture besides. I looked up ahead and there were Chet and old Art. They were going the other way.

"Hey, Chet!" I yelled. "Chet! Hey, Chet! The earth's round! It isn't flat at all!"

People started staring and laughing. I ducked into an alley and hurried on home.

The Report

THE FAMILY WAS ALREADY EATING. My mother was spooning something unrecognizable into Andrew's mouth.

"Good of you to drop in for a visit," my father said. "Why don't you stay for supper as long as you're here?"

"Thanks," I said. "It looks good."

"The chopped carrots are for Andrew," my father said. "Why don't you try the roast beef?"

After supper I hurried down to the drugstore with my roll of film and asked Mr. Spain to put a rush on it. Then I came back and started writing my report.

The next afternoon Chet said to me, "Wilfred Strathmore the Third turned in his project this morning. His father's secretary typed the report for him. She typed it on a high rag content bond paper. They sent it away and had it bound in limp leather. Wilfred Strathmore the Third's name is on it in big gold letters. The report is a hundred and seventy-five pages. Wilfred Strathmore the Third turned in his project a whole day before the deadline. He says he is a cinch to win that trip because the early bird gets the worm."

"Wilfred Strathmore the Third can have the worm," I said. "But I'm going to do my best to win that trip.

My report will be in by tomorrow. I am using a fifteen-cent ball point pen and white paper that has blue lines across it to write on and holes at the side so you can put it in a notebook. It is a black notebook that I got at the dime store. My report ought to run as much as maybe five or six pages if I write big."

That night I had my hands full. My official job was to stay with Andrew. But first I picked up my pictures. They were ready, and they were good. I could finish my report.

The report had three parts: (1) A mistake; (2) What was wrong; and (3) How the mistake was corrected and the right scientific answer arrived at.

I got up early the next morning and pasted up the pictures and diagrams. I pasted up the pictures in the same order I took them. First, the pictures from Halfway Point showing the mirage of Old Four Peaks. Then the pictures I took later from the same place without Old Four Peaks showing — along with the first diagram. And, last, the pictures I took from the top of Outlaw Rim with Old Four Peaks right where it had really been all the time — along with the second diagram.

When I had finished it and put it in a notebook, I went to Andrew's crib. "Andy, old boy," I said, "thanks for everything. I get a lot of things done while I'm hanging around here with you."

The Mistake

CHET AND OLD ART went with me to turn in my project report to Mr. Eggleston. As we walked along the hall toward Mr. Eggleston's room old Art said, "Listen, this is Pete's big day. A person doesn't turn in a big Original Outside Project like this every day in the week. Let's all celebrate. There's a swell movie at the Majestic. I've only seen it a few times. Come on. What do you say?"

"I would like to," I said. "But Mr. Eggleston gave us some review questions to study and I know my father will think they are important."

"Look," Chet said, "a person doesn't turn in a big Original Outside Project like this every day. Your father ought to understand that."

"Well, I'll see how things go," I said.

When I gave the notebook to Mr. Eggleston he said, "I'm glad you made it, Pete. This is the last day."

"Mr. Eggleston," I said, "about that review tomorrow. Do you suppose — well, I'd like to celebrate. A person doesn't turn in a big Original Outside Project like this every day. Do we have to have that quiz tomorrow? I know how Paul Revere warned everybody about the British. And I know about George Washington and people like that. I could learn the rest of it another time."

Mr. Eggleston stood up. He put the tips of his fingers together. "This *is* an important day for you and I *do* understand," he said. "But I'm afraid we can't interrupt the curriculum. Not even for this. The history of our nation is of vital importance to us all — especially its long and brave struggle for independence. Everybody knows about the midnight ride of Paul Revere, but I want my students to remember some of the other important events of those years. What our great leaders did then will stand for all time. We cannot mark too closely what they did for us and for the whole world."

"Yes, sir," I said.

When we were out in the hall, old Art said, "Gosh! I never thought of it like that."

"Look," Chet said, "why don't you do your studying *after* the show? We celebrate first. You study later."

"My father doesn't like movies when there is studying to do," I said. "But maybe I can go this one time."

My father wasn't home yet, so I explained everything to my mother. She said, "Well, Pete, this *is* a special occasion. Maybe it does call for a celebration. I don't mind if you go to the movie. You can eat dinner early and it won't be too late. But what about your homework?"

"There's only history," I said.

"History is important," she said. "When will you do the studying?"

"After the movie," I said.

"If that's a promise, you can go to the movie."

So Chet and old Art and I went to the movie. It was a double feature. One was a funny one about two fellows who joined a circus. One of them was a clown, only he was sad most of the time. The other one was a trapeze artist, only he was afraid of being up high. Finally they changed places and nobody found out about it for a long time. It was really funny.

The other picture was very serious. It was about a lady who went to college and when she graduated she went to New York so she could be a famous actress.

I did not see how it ended, because I went out to the popcorn machine for a little while.

Chet and old Art wanted to stay and see both pictures again. So did I. But I couldn't forget that homework. "I promised I would study my history lesson," I said.

Chet and old Art were pretty sore at me. "I thought we were going to celebrate," Chet whispered. People were beginning to look around at us. Chet whispers loud when he whispers.

I really did want to see it again, because you catch things the second time that you didn't catch the first time. So we agreed to stay for the first one again.

By the time I got home my father and mother were ready for bed. My mother came in to see where I had been. "Don't stay up too late, dear," she said finally. My father yelled good night to me from their room.

I was just about to settle down to study when I remembered that I hadn't had anything to eat since supper, except the popcorn. So I went down to the kitchen and made myself a peanut butter sandwich. After I ate the sandwich, I felt better, except that I was getting awfully sleepy.

"Maybe it would help just to stretch out for a little while," I thought. "I'll leave a light on so I won't go sound asleep."

The bed felt good. I fell asleep in a hurry. But after a

while I woke up. It was a good thing I left the light on.

I got up and splashed cold water in my face. Then I ran around the room in my stocking feet, lifting my knees high. After that I felt almost wide awake.

"Now for those history review questions," I said. I sat down and opened the notebook. What I saw made me jump out of the chair.

I flipped through the pages. There it was. My project report — the pictures, the diagrams. Everything.

I had given Mr. Eggleston the wrong notebook.

I felt numb all over. Practically a whole year shot! All that work for nothing! No trip to the Science Fair!

I knew they weren't fooling about the deadline. They had refused to accept Weldon Barlow's project the year before because it was a day late. They were very strict.

I felt like crying. But I was too mad. "Pete Sheldon," I said, "you fathead. You get a good project finished on time and then turn in the wrong notebook. Now you finally get around to looking at it — after it's too late."

Too late?

I thought a minute. The rules say the project has to be in by a certain day. But the day isn't over until midnight.

I looked at the clock. Eleven forty-five, fifteen minutes of the day left.

A lot of thoughts raced through my mind. I could call Mr. Eggleston. No. Calling wouldn't get the notebook to him. And calling might wake my mother and father. There wasn't time to talk to my father about this. I had to get my notebook to Mr. Eggleston before midnight. The Egglestons lived about three blocks away.

"No time to waste, Pete," I said.

I grabbed up the notebook and hurried down the stairs and out the front door.

Midnight

I RAN MOST OF THE WAY.

"Maybe Mr. Eggleston has to do homework, too," I told myself. "Maybe they're still up. Maybe they will even be glad to see me." But the block where they lived was dark. I stood on the sidewalk, breathing hard, and looked up at the big dark house.

I went up on the porch and pushed the doorbell. It sounded loud. I waited. I pushed the bell again. "Maybe they sleep in a part of the house far away from the door-bell," I thought. I knocked. Loud. Then waited. "Must be getting awfully close to midnight," I thought.

There was a noise somewhere. I couldn't tell whether it came from inside the house or not. "Maybe they went away," I thought. "Maybe they went somewhere for the night. Maybe this isn't even their house."

I rang the doorbell and knocked again. "Mr. Eggle-ston!" I called. "Mr. Eggleston! Mr. Eggleston!"

Something was moving in the house. A light went on inside. Then the porch light. I stood there blinking in the sudden brightness. Mr. Eggleston opened the door.

"It's almost midnight," I said.

"Are the British coming?" Mr. Eggleston asked.

"My project," I said. "The report — the notebook I

gave you today — it was the wrong one. My report's in this one." I held up the notebook.

"Come in," he said, yawning. He had on a long robe over his pajamas. The robe wasn't tied. It hung way down with the belt dragging on the floor.

We went into the living room and sat down on the sofa. Mr. Eggleston thumbed through the notebook. "This makes it official," he said. He looked at the big clock on the mantel. It was four minutes till midnight. "Looks like you just made it," he said.

"I'm awfully sorry to disturb you and Mrs. Eggleston," I said. "Thank you for letting me turn in my project like this. Thank you very much. I'm awfully sorry."

"No need to be sorry," he said. "I'm glad to know there's someone who cares this much about a school project — even an outside project."

I got up to go. "Uh, my homework," I said. "Those review questions. They're in that notebook I turned in today. If I can have it back now, I'll go study for the quiz."

"That notebook is locked in my desk at school," he said. "I don't have a list of the review questions here. But you've kept up your studies very well this year, Pete. Don't you think you remember the important points?"

"Well, Mr. Eggleston, I've been thinking about what you said today about how important history is. Especially the long fight for freedom. And besides, I promised my mother I would do my homework tonight. That was so she would let me go to the movie first. It was a double feature."

Mr. Eggleston yawned. "Yes, of course," he said. "But I'm sure your parents will understand. They're reasonable people, aren't they?"

"Well — uh — I — uh — well — "

"Now, Pete, surely you remember the important things in that history lesson. You can pass that quiz tomorrow." He yawned again.

"I guess I remember the important things pretty well," I said. "But I have trouble remembering when they happened. I get mixed up on dates."

"Well, now, dates aren't too terribly important," he said. "It's more important to know *why* the battles of Lexington and Concord took place on April 18, 1775."

"My dear, I'm sure it was April the nineteenth." It was Mrs. Eggleston. She was coming down the stairs. Her hair was in curlers. "Why, Pete Sheldon!" she said. "Isn't this awfully late for you to be up?"

"Yes, ma'am," I said.

"April nineteenth. Of course it was April nineteenth," Mr. Eggleston said, yawning. "I'm sleepy. It must be the hour. Pete doesn't have his homework questions. I locked his notebook in my desk at school."

"My dear, you shouldn't have done that," Mrs. Eggleston said. "I'll fix something for us and we'll talk about it."

She went off to the kitchen, and I could hear her slippers sliding on the linoleum.

"Now that business about the Boston Tea Party," Mr. Eggleston said. He took a book from the shelf and thumbed through it. "Here it is. This author has some very interesting things to say."

Mr. Eggleston started reading. His head nodded a few times, but he went on reading.

In a little while Mrs. Eggleston brought in a tray with milk, cookies and a pot of coffee. "We'll all feel better after some refreshments," she said. "Pete, how about a glass of milk and some cookies?"

"That would be fine," I said.

Mrs. Eggleston picked up the book. She looked through it while we ate. "History was always one of my very best subjects," she said. "I got higher grades in history than most of the other — My, but the jets are flying low tonight! I've been meaning to write to the City Council about that. Something is going to have to be done about — Oh, for goodness sake!"

It wasn't jets making that noise. Mr. Eggleston was snoring. His head was against the back of the sofa, and he looked peaceful and comfortable.

Mrs. Eggleston took off his slippers and lifted his feet onto the sofa. She put a cushion under his head and tucked the robe around his chin.

"There," she said. "Now, where were we? Oh, yes. Now. I think we can run over this lesson in a jiffy." We read through the chapter together, and I took notes.

When I was ready to leave I said, "Mrs. Eggleston, you are a very good teacher. I wish we had you at school."

She smiled and said, "Maybe sometime."

On the way home I got to thinking that I should have told my folks where I was going. "Maybe every light in the house will be on," I thought. "Maybe they'll have the whole town out looking for me." But when I got there, the house was dark and everything was quiet. Nobody had missed me.

I didn't turn on a light, and while I was getting ready for bed I bumped into a chair.

"That you, Pete? You still up?" my father called.

"I'm going to bed now," I said.

"Pretty late, isn't it, Pete? What've you been doing?"

"Studying history," I said.

Waiting

I<small>T WAS GOING TO BE</small> another whole week before they announced the winner. But there was a lot to do. The closer you come to the end of school, the more things you have to do and the less you have to learn.

Parents Day was that week. There were flowers in all of the rooms and everything was cleaned up until it looked as if no work was ever done there. Anyone who didn't know what usually went on would think we spent the whole year picking flowers and washing blackboards.

The parents came and met the teachers, and there were visitors everywhere. My mother and father shook hands with my teachers, and everybody laughed and talked about a lot of things. I didn't hear anybody say a word about work or studies or anything like that — anybody except Mr. Stroop, that is. I heard him talking to my father; and Mr. Stroop said, "I can truthfully say Pete's mind has been busy every minute."

Even with all the things to do, the week was long. But Friday finally came — the day they were going to announce the winner.

My stomach felt funny that morning. When I got to school I said to Chet, "I don't know if I really want that trip, or if I just want to get the suspense over with."

"Hey, look at this," Chet said. He pointed to an announcement on the bulletin board.

Because of the unusually large number of Original Outside Projects submitted this year, the judges have found it necessary to delay their decision for a few days. Winner of the trip to the State Science Fair will be announced in assembly on Monday morning.

"Chet," I said, "this is psychological warfare. That's what it is. Fiends! That's what they are."

"They can't do this to you," Chet said.

"I think this will be a long weekend," I said.

The time went even slower than I thought it would. On Saturday morning I loafed around the house and kept looking at the clock.

"Time will go faster if you keep busy," mother said.

"You're right," I said, and started for the yard. On the way out I glanced at the clock. Nine-fifteen.

First I tossed a basketball at the hoop on the garage door. Then I walked along the top of the back fence to see if I could balance as far as the Jones place. Then I oiled a wheel that had been sticking on one of my roller skates. Next I went down to the basement and threw darts for a while. Then I gave the basketball a few more tosses for good measure. I went in and looked at the clock. Nine twenty-seven. Twelve minutes had gone by.

I sat at the table with my chin in my hands and said to my mother, "Tell me when it's Monday morning."

My father came in while I was sitting there. "Well," he said, "what's this? I think we can do something about this situation."

We had a short talk, and he arranged for me to mow the lawn.

While I pushed the mower back and forth, I kept saying to myself, "Pete, the next time you haven't got anything to do, don't do it out in plain sight."

Decision

MONDAY MORNING FINALLY CAME.

In asembly I tried to be I-don't-care-about-it-at-all, as if I had never heard of any such thing as a trip to the State Science Fair.

Mr. Stroop made the announcement about the winner. He talked for quite a while about the fine talents and active young minds of the students.

He said the judges had taken into account the spirit in which the contestants approached their projects. And he said grades were an important consideration, too.

He said it had not been easy for the judges to make a choice, but one project stood out from all the others because of its unusual presentation.

I groaned and sank down in my seat. *Unusual presentation!* The leather cover! The gold printing! The hundred and seventy-five pages! "Chet," I said, "they're going to give that trip to Wilfred Strathmore the Third."

"Never mind, Pete," Chet said. "I think your project was the best, even if the judges don't think so."

Mr. Stroop was saying, "This one contestant had extreme confidence in the scientific approach. He had the courage to report first how he had made a mistake, then how the mistake was discovered, and finally, how the scientific answer was reached. The judges decided that its true scientific approach made this project the most original. They decided unanimously to award the prize for this project.

"It is my pleasure and privilege to announce that this year's Original Outside Project winner and recipient of the trip to the State Science Fair is — Peter Sheldon."

"Pete! That's you!" Chet yelled.

I didn't know what to do, so I just sat there while everybody clapped. I don't remember feeling anything much except a kind of tingling all over. I was really in a whirl.

After assembly Wilfred Strathmore the Third came over and shook my hand and said, "Congratulations, Pete."

I was still in such a whirl I couldn't think of anything to say except, "Thanks, Wilfred Strathmore the Third."

Expectations

THE SCIENCE FAIR WAS GREAT.

They had just about everything that has ever been invented in the modern world. There were electronic computers and all kinds of modern improvements.

They had a machine that could play chess. Somebody beat the machine two out of three games. The inventor is going to work on it some more so it can do better next time.

There was a big room almost bigger than our school gym. They called it The World of the Future. One of the things in it was a car that runs without a driver. It follows the road by itself while all the people in the car just sit around and talk and look at the billboards and scenery.

Besides that, in The World of the Future there was a big space ship for people who want to go to the moon and the planets and faraway places. And there was a smaller rocket ship to take people to all the countries in the world. This was for those who don't like to travel anywhere much at all.

Mr. Stroop came to the fair, too. We went around to the exhibits together. There was a house of the future that had a button in the wall, and when you pushed the button everything in the house worked automatically. Outside the house, too — even the lawn mower.

"How would you like to live in that house?" Mr. Stroop asked.

"Well, I don't know," I said. "If my family ever lived in a house like that, I'm pretty sure I know who would have to push the button."

They had places there where they were selling all kinds of useful things. A man was selling a combination potato peeler, bottle opener, thermometer, and weather forecaster. The man said it was guaranteed, so I bought one for my mother. She lets me use it any time I want to.

I use it mainly to see how hot the weather is. Twice in one week the weather report in the paper was wrong.

I talked to some of the people who ran the fair. I told them my ideas about scientific improvements in modern life. The people were all very nice, and I think they were really interested. But most of the ones I talked to said they didn't think there was any real need right now for bicycles with radar.

I talked to one man for a long time. He said scientific developments always take time and the hardest part of developing any new idea is convincing people it is a good thing.

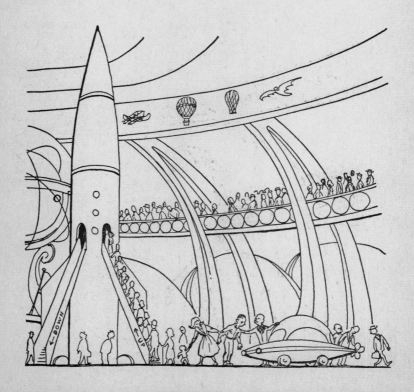

Looking at all those modern scientific improvements gave me some good ideas of my own. I'm working on a couple of them now.

I'll be a year older when school starts. I should be able to do even better than I did last year. They will probably be expecting bigger things of me there this year — especially Mr. Stroop and Mr. Eggleston and Mr. Henhauser.